# mary-kateandashley

## TWO of a kind™

### April Fools' Rules!

D0582590

# Look for these

# TWO of a kind™

## titles:

# mary-kateandashley

## TWO of a kind ™

# April Fools' Rules!

### by Judy Katschke

from the series created by Robert Griffard
& Howard Adler

📖 HarperCollins*Entertainment*
An Imprint of HarperCollinsPublishers

**A PARACHUTE PRESS BOOK**

## A PARACHUTE PRESS BOOK

Parachute Publishing, L.L.C.
156 Fifth Avenue
Suite 302
New York, NY 10010

First published in the USA by HarperEntertainment 2002
First published in Great Britain by HarperCollins*Entertainment* 2003
HarperCollins*Entertainment* is an imprint of HarperCollins*Publishers* Ltd,
77-85 Fulham Palace Road, Hammersmith, London, W6 8JB

The HarperCollins website address is
www.harpercollins.co.uk

1 3 5 7 9 10 8 6 4 2

The authors assert the moral right to be
identified as the authors of this work

ISBN 0 00 714463 6

Printed and bound in Great Britian by Clays Ltd, St Ives plc

# CHAPTER ONE

"I think I'm allergic to mornings," twelve-year-old Ashley Burke yawned as she squeezed some toothpaste onto her toothbrush.

"Me, too," Phoebe Cahill, Ashley's roommate, agreed. "Yesterday morning I was so tired, I almost washed my face with shampoo."

It was Monday morning and Ashley and Phoebe were in the bathroom at Porter House, getting ready for school. Porter House was their dorm at White Oak Academy, an all-girls boarding school in New Hampshire.

*BANG!*

Ashley jumped as the door to the bathroom burst open. "Oops," she said as she squirted toothpaste onto the mirror. She quickly wiped it off.

"Let's see what we have here," a girl's voice said.

Ashley turned to watch a dark-haired girl march into the bathroom with a clipboard. She wore charcoal-coloured trousers, a black sweater, and black boots.

"Who's she?" Ashley whispered to Phoebe as the girl peeked inside an empty shower cubicle.

"Some new first-form girl," Phoebe whispered back. "I saw her carrying bags into Marble Manor two days ago."

"Oh," Ashley said. She and her twin sister, Mary-Kate, knew what that was like. Earlier that year, they were the new kids at school.

*I'd better make her feel welcome*, Ashley thought. "Hi," she said cheerfully. "My name is Ashley, and this is my roommate—"

"Ah-ha!" the girl shouted, pointing to the shelf in the shower cubicle. "Just as I thought. There's no organic shampoo in this bathroom either!"

Phoebe peered over the rim of her blue-framed glasses. "Can we help you with something?"

The girl put her clipboard under her arm and reached out her hand. "Hi. I'm Lily Vanderhoff," she said, shaking hands with Ashley and Phoebe. "I used to go to the Rivington School in Vermont."

"Welcome to White Oak," Ashley said. "I think

you're really going to like it at this school."

"I hope so," Lily said. She hugged her clipboard and sighed. "At my old school, I always made changes around campus for the students. It looks like White Oak needs some changes, too!"

Lily turned and reached for the door handle. "Well, see you," she said. She swung open the door and marched out of the bathroom.

"What do you think she meant by 'changes'?" Phoebe asked.

"And what's wrong with our shampoo?" Ashley asked. "I like mine. It smells like strawberry-kiwi!"

Phoebe shrugged. "I guess we'll find out eventually," she said.

Ashley glanced at her watch and gasped. "Uh-oh," she said. "We'd better move it or we'll be late for morning announcements."

Other girls ran in and out of the bathroom as Ashley and Phoebe finished washing up. The two roommates hurried back to their room, got dressed, and raced to the auditorium for Mrs. Pritchard's daily announcement.

Mrs. Pritchard was the headmistress at White Oak. She was also known as The Head.

"Spring is in the air," Phoebe said as they hurried across campus. "I can't wait for warm weather."

Ashley nodded in agreement as her blonde hair whipped around in the breeze. It was the end of March and that meant longer days, budding trees – and long walks around campus with her boyfriend, Ross Lambert!

Ross was a student at the Harrington School for Boys down the road. The girls and boys shared some classes and clubs.

"At least we're not late," Phoebe said. She pulled open the door of the auditorium and the girls rushed inside.

"Look, there's Mary-Kate." Ashley hurried down the aisle and plopped into a seat next to her sister. Phoebe sat next to Ashley.

"What took you guys so long?" Mary-Kate asked them. "The Head will be out any minute."

"Phoebe and I were talking to a new girl," Ashley explained. She waved to her friends Cheryl Miller, Elise Van Hook and Campbell Scott, who were sitting on the other side of Mary-Kate.

"Really?" Mary-Kate asked, smiling. "What's her name?"

"Lily Vanderhoff," Ashley answered.

"We've already met her," Campbell said, leaning closer to Ashley. "Lily came into our bathroom with a clipboard yesterday afternoon."

"She complained that our soap wasn't vegetable-based," Elise added. "Whatever that means."

Mary-Kate glanced over Ashley's shoulder. "Here comes Lily now," she said.

Ashley turned and saw Lily walking down the aisle. She was still clutching her clipboard as she took a seat in the first row.

"I wonder why Lily switched schools right in the middle of term," Ashley said.

Mary-Kate's eyebrows shot up. "You mean you haven't heard?" she asked.

"Heard what?" Ashley replied.

"Lily is the daughter of Celia Vanderhoff," Campbell said. "The new head of the board of trustees."

"Wow," Ashley said, sitting back in her chair. The head of the board had more power than Mrs. Pritchard! "Well, we should try and be nice to her," she added. "It's tough being the new kid."

"I agree," Mary-Kate said.

Ashley watched as Mrs. Pritchard crossed the stage to the microphone stand. She was wearing a dark green suit with brown shoes.

"Good morning, girls," Mrs. Pritchard said brightly. "First I would like to announce that starting tomorrow, there will be a new kind of soap in the bathrooms."

Annoyed whispers filled the auditorium.

"It's an organic vegetable-based soap called Squeaky Green," Mrs. Pritchard explained.

"No way!" Ashley whispered. She stared at Lily beaming in the first row. "How did she do that?"

"I'll bet it's because her mom is the head of the board," Phoebe said.

Mrs. Pritchard shuffled some papers on the podium. "Next I have some exciting news to announce," she said. "It's the last week in March, which means it's that time of the year again."

Some girls in the second and third forms began to whisper to one another.

"What is she talking about?" Ashley asked Mary-Kate.

"I don't know," Mary-Kate replied. "But the older girls seem to think it's cool!" She pointed to the second- and third-formers.

"First-formers, this one's for you," Mrs. Pritchard said. "Are you ready for White Oak's biggest surprise?"

# CHAPTER TWO

Mary-Kate sat up in her seat. *What could it be?* she wondered.

"April Fools' Day is coming up," Mrs. Pritchard declared, "and it's one of White Oak's most important traditions."

"I love April Fools' Day!" Mary-Kate clasped her hands.

Mrs. Pritchard rested her elbows on the podium. "It all started back when I was a first-former at White Oak."

Mary-Kate smiled. It was hard to imagine Mrs. Pritchard when she was their age. What did she look like? Did she have a good report card? A boyfriend?

"There was a girl in my dorm named Olivia Farquar," Mrs. Pritchard went on. "The day before April Fools' Day, she sneaked into the laundry rooms of all the dorms with a jumbo box of starch."

Some of the older girls began to giggle.

"Starch makes clothing really stiff," Mrs. Pritchard explained, "so when Olivia dumped it into all the washing machines, our clothes wound up stiffer than frozen Popsicles!"

Mary-Kate laughed. She pictured Mrs. Pritchard and her classmates trying to sit down for morning announcements the next day. Their clothes were probably so stiff they couldn't even bend their legs!

Mrs. Pritchard chuckled. "When our head-mistress, Mrs. Sparrow, asked for an explanation, Olivia jumped up with a banner that said APRIL FOOLS!"

"That is the greatest prank," Ashley said.

"Every year since then," Mrs. Pritchard went on, "teams of first-formers have tried to top Olivia's prank. And slowly, it has become a White Oak tradition."

Mary-Kate sat straight up in her seat. *I'll bet I could top Olivia's prank,* she thought. She was a master prankster!

"So during the last week of March, White Oak holds a competition," Mrs. Pritchard continued. "I pick five girls from each first-form dorm to be part of a team. Those girls will be in charge of pulling pranks."

"I totally want to be one of those girls," Campbell said.

"Count me in," Elise added.

"The group of first-formers that pulls the best prank wins a prize for their dorm," Mrs. Pritchard said. "And this year that prize is – new furniture for their dorm's lounge!"

"No way!" Mary-Kate gasped.

"If any dorm could use new furniture, it's Porter House," Ashley whispered.

"Seriously," Cheryl added. "Those lumpy chairs were probably there since Mrs. Pritchard was a student."

"We have two restrictions on the pranks," Mrs. Pritchard explained. "They can't hurt anyone, and they can't interfere with your schoolwork."

As Mrs. Pritchard explained a few more details, the girls chatted excitedly.

"I would make the best prankster," Cheryl said.

"So would I!" Phoebe added.

"Me, too," Ashley chimed in.

Everyone stared at Ashley. "You want to be on the team?" Cheryl asked.

"Sure," Ashley said. "Why wouldn't I?"

"I guess we've just never seen you pull a prank before," Campbell explained.

"What do you mean?" Ashley argued. "Remember when I sent that pizza to snooty Dana Woletsky and her friends? The one with the slimy rubber worms?"

"Hey, that was my idea!" Mary-Kate said. "Your pranks are the ones that always backfire."

"Oh . . . right," Ashley said slowly.

"Remember that time you put a rubber spider in my water glass?" Phoebe asked. "But then you wound up drinking out of it by accident and scaring yourself?"

"Oops," Ashley said. "I forgot about that one. But what about the time I wanted to sneak around the dorm and take everyone's shoes?"

"But that was too hard to pull off," Cheryl said. "How would we carry shoes from thirty girls? And besides, it wasn't that funny!"

"I thought it was funny," Ashley muttered.

"It's not like we wouldn't want you on the team," Mary-Kate explained. "We're just surprised that you'd want to be part of it. I mean, with your track-record and everything."

"I guess you're right," Ashley said slowly. She shrugged. "I don't really want to be on the team anyway."

"All right, girls," Mrs. Pritchard called out. "I'll start with Porter House. Please raise your hand if you want to be on the team."

Mary-Kate, Cheryl, Elise, Phoebe and Campbell shot their hands into the air.

"It looks like the five of you have it," Mrs. Pritchard said, pointing to Mary-Kate and her friends.

"Yay!" the girls cheered, hugging one another.

Mrs. Pritchard went on to choose the teams from Phipps House and Marble Manor. Soon, excited whispers filled the auditorium.

"Settle down, girls," Mrs. Pritchard said, waving her arms. "I have some more good news to share. White Oak and Harrington also celebrate April Fools' Day with a Backward Banquet in our dining hall. That's where the meal starts with dessert and ends with soup."

"Dessert first?" Campbell whispered. She rubbed her hands together. "That's a tradition I could get used to!"

"And," Mrs. Pritchard continued, "two days before the banquet, Harrington and White Oak have tryouts for a King and Queen of Fools. The king and queen are treated like royalty at the banquet."

"What do we have to do to try out?" a girl in the first row asked.

11

"The official rules for the pranking competition and the Queen of Fools competition will be posted outside my office," Mrs. Pritchard explained. "That's it for morning announcements. Good luck to the contestants!"

"We are so going to win this contest," Cheryl announced as everyone stood up. "On April Fools' Day last year I sneaked into my older brother's room while he was sleeping and polished his toenails bubble gum pink."

"You call that a prank?" Campbell said. "In fourth grade I put a whoopie cushion on my teacher's chair!"

"Did she laugh?" Elise asked.

"Nope." Campbell grinned. "But I sure thought it was funny!"

"I've pulled some awesome pranks, too," Mary-Kate bragged. "And I can definitely do it again."

*Olivia Farquar,* Mary-Kate thought, *you are about to meet your match!*

# CHAPTER THREE

"New furniture in the lounge!" Ashley said on the breakfast line that morning. "Do you think Mrs. Pritchard will let us pick it out?"

"Picture it," Mary-Kate said, sliding her tray past the muffins. "We could have beanbag chairs—"

"With animal-print pillows," Elise added.

"And big posters of 4-You," Campbell finished. 4-You was their favourite boy band.

The girls grabbed containers of milk and juice as they inched their way towards the end of the line.

"Well, one thing's for sure," Mary-Kate said. "We're going to win!"

The girls stopped in front of the metal oatmeal trays. Having flavoured oatmeal every morning was another cherished tradition at White Oak.

"What are the flavours for today?" Phoebe asked.

Mary-Kate stepped up to read the sign. "Banana walnut and Rocky Road," she answered. "Yum!"

"Banana walnut?" a voice cried out. "Rocky Road? Are you serious?"

Mary-Kate whirled around. Lily Vanderhoff was standing in line behind them.

"Don't you like banana walnut and Rocky Road, Lily?" Mary-Kate asked.

"Flavoured oatmeal is a tradition here at White Oak," Ashley explained.

"That's cool if oatmeal is a tradition," Lily explained. "But unless it's served in its purest form, it's really not good for you."

Mary-Kate gulped. "You mean you want to serve it . . . plain?"

Lily nodded. "All those flavours add artificial yucky preservatives to the oatmeal. You don't want to eat that, do you?"

"If it makes it taste good," Ashley said, "then why not!"

Lily sighed. She pulled the clipboard from her purple backpack and wrote something down. Then she picked up her tray and walked over to a table on the other side of the dining hall.

"You guys," Elise asked slowly, "you don't think Lily will do away with flavoured oatmeal, do you?"

"Nah," Mary-Kate said. "Even the board of trustees can't resist banana walnut and Rocky Road!"

The girls grabbed bowls of steaming hot oatmeal and headed for an empty table. As they did, Mrs. Pritchard entered the room and called for silence.

"I have a quick announcement to make," Mrs. Pritchard said. "In addition to our new soap, we'll be using organic shampoo as well. Carry on."

"Gee," Ashley grumbled. "Lily sure made that change fast."

"Someone should talk to her," Campbell said. "She's going to have a lot of enemies at White Oak if she doesn't stop changing things around here."

"I'll say something to her," Ashley volunteered. "I'll go over to her table right after breakfast."

"Thanks, Ashley," Mary-Kate said as everyone put down their trays. "So, team, let's talk about our prank. What is it going to be?"

"I don't know," Phoebe said. "But whatever it is, I'll bet we'll go down in White Oak history for it!"

"I can see it now," Elise added. "A plaque for the greatest pranksters at White Oak in the main hall – with all five of our names on it!"

Ashley slumped a little in her seat. *But my name*

*won't be on the plaque with everyone else's,* she thought.

As her friends chatted about different pranks they could play, Ashley quickly finished her breakfast.

"I'll go talk to Lily now," she said. She stood up, but saw that Lily had already left the dining hall.

"I guess I'll catch up with her later," Ashley said. But her friends weren't listening to her. They were too busy talking about pranks. And the more they did, the more Ashley felt left out.

*I should have raised my hand to be on the April Fools' team,* Ashley thought as she plodded across campus after breakfast. *I know I would have come up with some great pranks. And my shoe prank* was *funny!*

"Yo, Ashley!" a boy's voice called out.

Ashley glanced over her shoulder and saw her cousin, Jeremy, running towards her. Twelve-year-old Jeremy Burke was a student at Harrington. He was also the family jokester and a big pain!

"What are you doing here?" Ashley asked when Jeremy caught up with her.

"I heard they were setting up an ice cream bar in the student union," Jeremy said, licking his lips.

He fell into step beside Ashley. "What's up?" he asked. "You're even more boring than usual."

Ashley sighed. "All my friends were picked to be on the April Fools' team," she explained. "I guess after hearing them talk about it I feel a little left out."

"There are other ways to have fun on April Fools' Day without being on some dumb team," Jeremy said.

"Oh, yeah?" Ashley asked. "How?"

"You could run for Queen of Fools," Jeremy answered.

Ashley remembered what Mrs. Pritchard had said about the king and queen tryouts. "That's right," she said slowly. "I was so focused on pranking, I never thought about becoming queen!"

"You'd make a great Queen of Fools," Jeremy said.

Ashley stopped walking. "Hmm. What do I have to do to try out?" she asked.

"You have to tell jokes," Jeremy replied. "I'll bet you could win. What's your best joke?"

"How about the one I told last Thanksgiving?" Ashley asked. "Why do turkeys make great musicians? Because they carry their drumsticks wherever they go!"

Jeremy rolled his eyes.

"How about this one. If the number two pencil is so great, why isn't it number one?" Ashley grinned.

Jeremy stuck his finger in his mouth and pretended to gag. "I think you need some help from the master," he said, pointing to his chest.

"No thanks," Ashley said. "I can do it on my own."

Jeremy put a hand on Ashley's shoulder. "Trust me. You can't. You're not funny enough!"

"Yes, I am!" Ashley argued. "I don't need your help." She started to walk away.

Jeremy shrugged. "That's too bad," he said. "Because I heard that everyone is voting for Ross to be king."

"Ross?" Ashley asked. She stopped walking and turned to face her cousin. "As in my boyfriend, Ross?"

Jeremy nodded. "I heard him telling some jokes in the dining hall the other day. The guys laughed so hard they sprayed milk all over the table."

"Gross," Ashley said, wrinkling her nose.

"Well, the guys thought Ross was so funny that they convinced him to run for king," Jeremy said.

Ashley clasped her hands to her chest. She could see it now – she and Ross, sitting side by side with golden crowns on matching thrones. It was perfect!

"You know what?" Ashley told Jeremy. "If Ross is going to be king, then there's only one girl who should be queen – and that's me."

She folded her arms across her chest. "You just wait. I'm going to win that competition."

# CHAPTER FOUR

"How about we pull a prank on Dana?" Cheryl suggested on Tuesday afternoon. The Porter House team was hanging out in Mary-Kate and Campbell's room.

"We'll replace all of her supercool outfits with really ugly clothes," Cheryl went on.

"What kind of ugly clothes?" Elise asked, hugging a pillow.

"You know," Cheryl said, "polyester bell-bottom trousers, saddle shoes—"

"Hey!" Phoebe interrupted. "You're talking about my entire wardrobe."

Mary-Kate giggled. Phoebe loved anything that was vintage. In fact her wardrobe was filled to the brim with clothes from second-hand shops.

"We should definitely play a prank on Phipps House," Elise chimed in. "I heard that Dana and her friends are on the team. They deserve it." Dana Woletsky was the snobbiest girl in the first form.

"Everyone in our dorm has been begging us to win," Mary-Kate said, swivelling around in her desk chair. "Talk about pressure!"

"I know," Cheryl agreed, leaning back on Campbell's bed. "This morning Wendy Linden insisted I had to win new furniture for the dorm."

"And Samantha Kramer told me everyone is expecting us to make Porter House number one," Campbell put in.

"I'm sure we can do it," Mary-Kate said. "But April Fools' Day is Saturday," she went on, "which means we have only four days to think of a super-brilliant prank. So first – we have to get organised."

"I have an idea," Campbell said.

"An idea for a prank?" Phoebe asked.

Campbell shook her head. "No, a way to get organised," she said. "Every team I ever belonged to had a captain. So, what if we had one, too?"

"Like who?" Mary-Kate asked.

"Like you," Campbell replied.

"Me?" Mary-Kate squeaked. "Why me?"

"Because," Campbell said, "you'll take charge of the situation and make sure we actually get stuff done."

"You're a great motivator," Elise pointed out. "You can definitely get us to agree on a prank."

"I think Mary-Kate would make a great captain," Phoebe said. "Those of you who elect Mary-Kate as captain of the Porter House team, raise your hands."

Mary-Kate watched as each of her teammates raised one hand. *How awesome!* she thought.

"I accept." Mary-Kate jumped to her feet. "And as your captain I promise to lead us all to victory. I promise to beat Phipps and Marble Manor and bring Olivia Farquar to her knees!"

"Yeah!" Cheryl cheered.

Mary-Kate waved everyone into a tighter circle. "Okay, team," she said. "It's time to get serious."

"What should we do?" Campbell asked.

"Let's talk about the best tricks that were ever played on us," Mary-Kate said. "Maybe that will give us some ideas."

Everyone was silent for a moment.

"One time I was invited to a sleepover," Cheryl said. "The invitation said to show up in your PJs."

"And?" Phoebe asked.

"I wore my flannel PJs with the green polka

dots," Cheryl explained. "But when I got to the party, girls and boys were there wearing regular clothes. The joke was totally on me!"

"How embarrassing." Elise covered her mouth with one hand.

"Is there any way we can pull off a trick like that?" Mary-Kate asked.

"You mean get the girls in Phipps to wear their pyjamas all day?" Cheryl said. "How would we do that?"

Mary-Kate snapped her fingers. "I know! We can put fliers in the Phipps mailbox telling everyone to come to morning announcements in their pyjamas."

"We can write on the fliers that tomorrow is an annual lazy day," Elise suggested.

"Except the only lazy ones will be the girls from Phipps," Cheryl added with a smile.

"Brilliant, Mary-Kate," Phoebe said.

"See? I told you she'd make a great team captain," Campbell said.

"Thanks, you guys," Mary-Kate said. "We're going to score tons of points with this one." She started a round of high-fives. "Let's do it!"

"Did you print up the fliers?" Mary-Kate asked Phoebe outside the main office later that day.

"Yup," Phoebe answered in a low voice. She pulled a stack of purple papers from her backpack. "I used the printer in the *Acorn* office. Being on the staff of the school newspaper has its perks."

Mary-Kate grinned. "Okay, Phoebe. You keep Mrs. Cathcart busy while I shove the fliers into the Phipps mailbox." Mrs. Cathcart was the secretary in the main office.

"No problem." Phoebe handed Mary-Kate the purple fliers and entered the office. "Hi, Mrs. Cathcart," she told the secretary. "Wow! Is that an authentic 1950s mohair sweater you're wearing?"

"Yes, it is," Mrs. Cathcart replied. "How did you know?"

"Because I have one just like it," Phoebe replied, turning Mrs. Cathcart away from the mailboxes. "Where did you get yours?"

While Phoebe and Mrs. Cathcart talked about the sweater, Mary-Kate sneaked into the office and hurried to a row of metal boxes where the mail was sorted for each dorm.

"Oh, dear!" Mary-Kate heard Mrs. Cathcart say. "Is it five o'clock already? I'd better finish handing out the mail."

Mary-Kate gasped. She quickly scanned the boxes until she saw one marked PH. "Phipps

House. There it is," she whispered. Mary-Kate threw the purple papers into the box and slipped out of the office before the secretary could see her.

Mission accomplished!

"Mary-Kate! We're late!"

"Mmmph?" Mary-Kate grunted. She was having the most awesome dream. A marble statue of Olivia Farquar was being removed from the centre of campus – and replaced with a statue of Mary-Kate!

"Mary-Kate, wake up," Campbell said. "I forgot to set the alarm clock. We're going to miss morning announcements."

Morning announcements? The words made Mary-Kate leap out of bed.

It was Wednesday morning. That meant that in a little while, the Phipps girls were going to march into the auditorium in their pyjamas. And Mary-Kate didn't want to miss that!

Mary-Kate crossed the room to the wardrobe. She stepped on a piece of bright purple paper that had been slipped under the door.

"That's funny." Mary-Kate picked up the sheet. "That's the same colour Phoebe used for our fliers."

"Is that . . . ?" Campbell began as Mary-Kate read the flier.

"Campbell!" Mary-Kate cried. "It's our flier!"

"What is it doing here?" Campbell yelled. "You put them in the Phipps mailbox, right?"

"I-I think so," Mary-Kate stammered, trying to remember. "I put them in the box marked PH. That stands for Phipps House, right?"

"Oh, no!" Campbell groaned. "Mary-Kate, PHH is for Phipps House. PH is for Porter House!"

Mary-Kate froze. "I was in such a hurry, I didn't think of that," she replied.

Campbell pulled on Mary-Kate's arm. "Come on, we have to warn everybody!" She pulled open the door and ran into the hallway.

Mary-Kate followed Campbell. "Open up!" she shouted, knocking on the next door. But nobody answered.

Campbell banged on some more doors. Then she ran down the hall and peeked into the bathroom. "No one's in here," she cried. "Everyone already left for morning announcements!"

Mary-Kate rushed back into their room and over to the window. She pulled back the curtain.

"There's a girl walking out of Porter House with her pyjamas on," Mary-Kate reported. "Which means we just played a prank on our own dorm!"

# CHAPTER FIVE

"I'm so sorry, guys," Mary-Kate said in the auditorium that morning. She had just finished telling Ashley and the rest of her teammates about the mix-up.

Ashley scanned the room. Dozens of Porter House girls were dressed in their pyjamas. Some even wore fuzzy slippers. "It's not that many girls," she said, trying to be helpful.

The Porter House team stared at Ashley.

Ashley shrugged. "Okay, maybe it is."

Mrs. Pritchard walked onto the stage. "Good morning, girls," she said. Then she gazed curiously around the auditorium. "Why are there so many girls dressed in pyjamas?"

# April Fools' Rules!

A surprised Porter House girl stood up. She was wearing flannel pyjamas decorated with teacups.

"We all got fliers this morning, Mrs. Pritchard," she explained. "They said today was a lazy day."

Other Porter House girls nodded.

"Lazy day?" Mrs. Pritchard repeated. Then she began to laugh. "Whose brilliant April Fools' Day prank was that?"

"Should we tell her it was ours?" Phoebe whispered.

"No way," Mary-Kate whispered back. "The last thing we want is for everyone to know we played a prank on our own dorm."

"Mary-Kate is right," Elise whispered. "If we admit to tricking ourselves, we'll really look like fools!"

Mrs. Pritchard folded her hands on the podium. "Phipps team?" she asked. "Was this your prank?"

Ashley sat up in her seat. Dana Woletsky and her teammates were whispering to each other. Finally, Dana stood up. "Yes, Mrs. Pritchard," she said sweetly. "We pulled the pyjama prank."

Ashley gasped. "They're taking credit for your prank!"

"How could they?" Campbell asked, shaking her head.

"Congratulations to Phipps House," Mrs. Pritchard said. "I'll talk to the voting committee about your prank. But I'll tell you now – it sure was a good one!"

Mary-Kate slumped in her seat. Slowly, she turned to Ashley. "Boy," she whispered, "some team leader I'm turning out to be."

"Our first announcement this morning," Mrs. Pritchard went on, "is that we will no longer be serving flavoured oatmeal in the dining hall. We have realised that oatmeal should be kept in its purest form."

Ashley's mouth fell open. "Lily did it again," she said to her friends. "I promise, guys – I'm going to talk to her the next chance I get!"

"I totally let my team down," Mary-Kate said later that day. She and Ashley were hanging out in the student union discussing the prank. "We had this awesome idea and I blew it."

Ashley sat back on her beanbag chair. "You'll get them next time," she said. "And you'll get back at Phipps for stealing your idea. That was so uncool."

"But our next prank has to be even better than that one," Mary-Kate sighed. "Got any ideas?"

"No," Ashley replied, "but I do have some exciting news to tell you. I found another way to be a part of April Fools' Day."

Mary-Kate's face brightened. "Really?" she said. "How?"

"I'm trying out for Queen of Fools," Ashley replied.

"That sounds like fun," Mary-Kate said, leaning forward. "If you become queen, will you get to wear a beautiful gown?"

"Definitely," Ashley said. "And a gold crown, I bet."

"Awesome," Mary-Kate said.

"But first I have to win the competition," Ashley said.

"What do you have to do?" Mary-Kate asked.

"I have to tell jokes at a White Oak assembly," Ashley explained. "The funniest girl will be voted queen."

"Then you'd better get started on a routine," Mary-Kate said. "Did you think of any good jokes yet?"

"Well," Ashley replied, "I've been collecting jokes from inside the Palooka bubble gum wrappers since yesterday."

Mary-Kate laughed. "Those always crack me up," she said.

The door of the student union swung open. Lily walked in by herself.

"Let's invite Lily to hang out with us," Ashley said. "She probably has no one to sit with."

"Yeah," Mary-Kate agreed. "And we can talk to her about not changing things around."

Ashley waved to Lily. "Hi!" she called.

"Hi, guys," Lily said, rushing over to Mary-Kate and Ashley. "I am really upset."

"Why?" Mary-Kate asked.

"Did you know that the laundry service uses artificial fabric softener on our laundry?" Lily asked.

"So?" Ashley replied. "It makes our clothes nice and soft."

Lily shook her head. "We should never put that stuff near our skin. It's loaded with chemicals. I'm going to have to do something about it."

"But—" Ashley started to say.

"See you!" Lily turned and rushed out.

"Now she wants to fix our fabric softener?" Mary-Kate frowned. "We didn't even get the chance to tell her that we didn't like her other changes!"

"I know," Ashley replied. "At this rate she'll change the name of our dorm by the end of the week!"

"At least she hasn't changed anything about

**30**

April Fools' Day yet," Mary-Kate said. "So tell me some more about the Queen of Fools."

"Well, the best part is that the King of Fools is probably going to be Ross!" Ashley said.

Mary-Kate smiled. "Well, here comes King Ross now."

Ashley turned in her chair and saw Ross walking towards them. He was wearing jeans and a dark green sweater.

She grinned. Ross's floppy brown hair was so cute!

"Hey," Ross said. He gave Ashley a hug. "I thought I'd find you here."

"Well, I've got to go," Mary-Kate said, standing up. "It's time to come up with the perfect prank."

"If anyone can do it, it's you," Ashley said. "Good luck!"

Mary-Kate waved and left the union.

Ross plopped down into the empty beanbag chair next to Ashley. "So, what's up?"

"Not much, your majesty," Ashley said.

"Huh?" Ross asked. "What do you mean, 'your majesty'?"

"I heard that you're going to try out for King of Fools," Ashley said.

"Yup," Ross said. "But I'm not exactly on the throne yet."

Ashley leaned forward in her chair. "Want to try out some of your jokes on me?" she asked.

Ross shrugged. "Okay," he said. "How about this one. The United States Army just announced their new secret weapon . . . my roommate's gym socks!"

Ashley laughed. "Funny."

"Here's another," Ross said. "New England has great seafood restaurants. I went into one and asked them if they served crabs. The waiter said, 'We serve anyone, sir. Have a seat!'"

Ashley laughed again. "Those are great. You'll definitely be chosen for king."

"You think?" Ross said.

"I know!" Ashley insisted. "Won't it be great when you're king and I'm queen of the Backward Banquet?"

Ross's eyebrows shot up. "You're running for queen?" he asked.

Ashley frowned. "Why do you sound so surprised?" she asked. *Does Ross think I'm not funny?* she wondered.

Ross cleared his throat. "Um, Ashley—" he began.

"Yo, Ross!" a boy's voice called out.

Ashley turned her head. Ross's roommate, Jason Quintero, was peeking through the front door.

"What's going on?" Ross asked.

"That volcano you built in the science lab is oozing all over our room," Jason said.

"Uh-oh," Ross said. He turned to Ashley. "Gotta go. See you later!"

"Later," Ashley said cheerfully as she watched Ross leave the student union. But inside she didn't feel so cheerful.

*It sure sounded like Ross doesn't want me to try out for queen,* Ashley thought. *I wonder why?*

# CHAPTER SIX

"It's study period, Mary-Kate," Cheryl complained. "Why did you drag us all the way to the bathroom in Porter House?"

Mary-Kate leaned against the sink. "To announce my idea for our next prank," she said.

Everyone watched Mary-Kate pull a box out of her backpack. It was temporary hair colour called Hue Go Girl. The model on the box had bright green hair.

"Ta-daaa!" Mary-Kate sang.

"What are we going to do with that?" Phoebe asked.

"I'm glad you asked," Mary-Kate said. "As we all know, thanks to Lily Vanderhoff, everyone at

White Oak is using the same organic shampoo."

"Yeah, and it smells like cauliflower," Cheryl added, pinching her nose.

"So I was thinking," Mary-Kate went on, "we could pour temporary green hair colour into a bunch of shampoo bottles. Then we can sneak them into the bathrooms at Phipps."

Elise gasped. "So when the Phipps girls wash their hair, they'll really be colouring it instead!"

"But isn't that mean?" Phoebe asked.

"No way." Mary-Kate pointed to the box. "See, it says it washes right out."

"But won't everyone notice that the shampoo in the bottles is green?" Phoebe asked.

"The organic shampoo bottles are made of dark brown plastic," Mary-Kate said. "So no one should notice the green stuff."

"Why don't we make the switch in one of our rooms?" Campbell asked.

"That might get messy," Cheryl replied. "We should just do it in here."

"But what if someone comes in while we're making the switch?" Campbell went on.

"Not a problem," Mary-Kate said. She pulled a piece of paper and a marker out of her backpack. Then she wrote Out of Order – Please Use First

Floor Bathroom on the paper. "I'll just tape this on the door until we're done."

"Mary-Kate, you think of everything," Phoebe said.

"That's why she's our team captain," Campbell pointed out.

Mary-Kate blushed. Her teammates were being so nice to her – even after she totally messed up the last prank. She *had* to lead them to victory!

Mary-Kate stuck the paper on the outside of the door while the other girls poured the green hair colour into the bottles.

"Next period is starting soon," Mary-Kate said, glancing at her watch. "Why don't we come back during dinner and pull the switch then?"

The girls agreed. Mary-Kate placed the shampoo bottles in a cabinet near the sink and shut the door. Then the girls hurried out of the bathroom.

"I can't wait to see Dana Woletsky with green hair," Campbell laughed.

"And when she realises it was because of our prank," Mary-Kate joked, "she'll be even greener with envy!"

"They're gone!" Mary-Kate gasped as she peeked into the bathroom cabinet a few hours later.

"Where could they be?" Cheryl cried. The girls searched the bathroom for the shampoo bottles.

Elise pushed aside a shower curtain. "I found one!" she called.

"There's one in here, too!" Campbell called from inside the next cubicle.

Mary-Kate sprinted into one of the empty cubicles and picked up the brown shampoo bottle from the ledge. When she tipped it over, green hair dye trickled out.

"How did this happen?" Mary-Kate wailed. "There were three full bottles of shampoo on the shelves when we left. Why would anyone take the bottles out of the cabinet?"

The bathroom door swung open. Two other girls from Porter House walked in.

"Hi, team," Cindy Patino said. "How's the prank coming along?"

"Remember," Suzanne Cole said, "Porter House is counting on you."

Mary-Kate stared at the girls. Then, without a word, she dashed out of the bathroom. Her teammates followed her.

"Don't use the shampoo!" Campbell called over her shoulder to Cindy and Suzanne.

"Mary-Kate, where are we running to?" Elise panted.

"The dining hall," Mary-Kate replied. "We have to see how much damage was done!"

The girls skidded into the dining hall. "Do you see what I see?" Phoebe asked.

"Unfortunately," Mary-Kate groaned.

On the serving line were five girls from Porter House – and all of them had bright green hair!

Mary-Kate went over to a girl named Lauren who lived on her floor. "Hi, Lauren," she said. "What happened to your hair?"

"Someone put hair colour in the shampoo bottles," Lauren replied with a frown. "What I want to know is, why does everyone keep playing April Fools' pranks on Porter House?"

"Um, yeah . . . me, too," Mary-Kate said, even though she already knew the answer. "So how did it happen? Was the bottle on the shower shelf?"

"There were no shampoo bottles on the shelves," Lauren explained. "The other girls and I opened the cabinet and found some more."

"Well, I wouldn't worry," Mary-Kate said. "I bet it washes out right away."

"It better!" Lauren said.

Mary-Kate ran back to her teammates, who were huddled at a table in the corner.

"Mary-Kate," Elise said, shaking her arm.

"You're not going to believe what we just heard."

"Some girls from Marble Manor were talking about their team's prank," Phoebe said. "They said they sneaked into all the Porter House bathrooms and stole our shampoo!"

"That must be why there was no shampoo on the shelves when Lauren went in there," Mary-Kate said.

Mrs. Pritchard came through the dining hall doors. "Can I have everyone's attention!" she called. "I wanted to announce that from now on, we'll be using herbal fabric softener in our laundry."

Mary-Kate groaned. "Lily . . . again!"

"I thought Ashley was going to say something to her," Cheryl said.

"We tried to talk to her in the student union," Mary-Kate said. "But she walked away before we could say anything! Don't worry. I'm sure Ashley will say something soon."

"Oh, my," Mrs. Pritchard said, looking at the green-headed girls. "How did this happen?"

"Someone put green stuff in our shampoo," Lauren said.

"Looks like an April Fools' prank to me," Mrs. Pritchard said. She turned to the rows of tables. "Did any of the April Fools' teams play a prank involving shampoo?"

"We did, Mrs. Pritchard," Kendra Rosenblatt from Marble Manor called out.

"Well done, Marble Manor!" Mrs. Pritchard said. "I do believe that prank will go over really well with the voting committee."

While Marble Manor cheered, the Porter House team stared blankly at one another.

"But it was our prank!" Elise cried.

"Until it backfired," Cheryl muttered.

Mary-Kate's heart sank into her stomach. How could this happen . . . again?

# CHAPTER SEVEN

"Wait until you hear these jokes," Ashley told Mary-Kate. "You are going to crack up!"

Mary-Kate sighed. "After what happened today, I could use a good laugh."

It was Wednesday night and Ashley had invited Mary-Kate to her room to listen to her routine.

"Go ahead," Mary-Kate said. She sat cross-legged on Ashley's rug and leaned against her bed.

"I wanted to find out if time flies," Ashley said, "so I threw my alarm clock!"

Mary-Kate laughed weakly.

*Not exactly the response I was hoping for*, Ashley thought. "Okay, here's the next one," she said. "I knew there was an elephant in my refrigerator when I found his footprints in the butter."

Mary-Kate didn't laugh. Instead, she raised her eyebrows.

*Maybe she didn't get it,* Ashley thought. "When I found his footprints in—" she repeated.

"The butter!" Mary-Kate said. "I've heard that one before. What else do you have?"

Ashley told a few more jokes. But all she got out of Mary-Kate was an occasional chuckle.

Ashley planted her hands on her hips. "What's the matter?" she asked. "Don't you think I'm funny?"

"Well . . ." Mary-Kate hesitated. "Your jokes might need some work."

Ashley paced her room. "If my jokes aren't funny, I'll lose the crown to someone else!" she complained. "If Ross is going to be king, then I *have* to be queen."

"Maybe you just need a little help," Mary-Kate suggested.

Ashley sat down next to her sister. "From who?" she asked. "Who do we know with tons of funny jokes?"

As soon as she asked the question, Ashley groaned. She knew someone who had lots of funny jokes. And it was the last person she wanted to ask!

\*        \*        \*

"I can't believe I'm doing this," Ashley muttered as she made her way across the student union. She spotted her cousin playing a Mice from Mars video game.

"Hi, Jeremy," Ashley said, coming up behind him.

"Ahhh!" Jeremy shouted through clenched teeth. He glared at Ashley. "You just hurled my spaceship millions of light years off course!"

"Sorry," Ashley said.

"What do you want?" Jeremy asked.

Ashley took a deep breath. She didn't want to ask her cousin for help. But she had no choice!

"I'm trying out for Queen of Fools tomorrow," Ashley said. "And I need . . . some guidance."

Jeremy leaned against the video game and grinned. "So, you finally realised that you desperately need my help?"

Ashley clenched her fists. "No," she insisted. "I'm not desperate."

"Oh, really?" Jeremy asked.

"Okay," Ashley admitted. "So I'm desperate. I just need a few pointers."

"In other words, you want me to share my jokes with you?" Jeremy asked.

Ashley slowly nodded.

"Sorry," Jeremy said, sticking his hands in his pockets. "But if I remember correctly, you said you didn't want my help. You were going to do it all by yourself."

Ashley watched as Jeremy pulled a Gooey Chewy bar from his pocket. Her cousin was always eating something. That gave her an idea. "What if I buy you some quarter-pounders tomorrow at the Burger Hut?" she asked.

Jeremy's eyes lit up. "The Burger Hut?" he repeated. "Throw in a chocolate shake and jumbo fries and you've got a deal."

Ashley sighed. "Deal," she said.

Jeremy plugged two more quarters into the video game. "See you at Burger Hut," he said as he started playing again.

*Boy,* Ashley thought as she walked away. *What a girl has to do to become a queen!*

"Are you ready?" Mary-Kate asked Ashley. It was Thursday night and the girls were backstage at the Queen of Fools competition.

Ashley nodded. "I have a whole bunch of new jokes," she said.

"So Jeremy came through?" Mary-Kate asked.

Ashley sighed. "After three burgers, two large

orders of fries, a jumbo shake . . . and a huge burp!"

"Yuck!" Mary-Kate cried. "Want to practise a few jokes on me before the show?"

"Okay," Ashley agreed, and told her sister two jokes.

Mary-Kate cracked up. "Those are great!" she said. "You're going to bring down the house."

"You think so?" Ashley asked. "I'm still really nervous."

"You'll be wonderful," Mary-Kate replied. "Well, I guess I should find a seat in the audience." With a little wave, Mary-Kate made her way to a seat in the third row near her teammates.

Ashley ran through the rest of her act in her head. *Maybe Mary-Kate is right,* she thought, growing a little more confident. *Maybe my jokes* are *good.*

"Name?" a voice interrupted Ashley's thoughts.

"Huh?" Ashley turned and saw Vicky Arroyo, a third-former. She was wearing a headset and holding a clipboard. "Oh, I'm Ashley Burke."

"You're on second," Vicky said, writing something on her clipboard. "After Brandy Oliver."

"Okay," Ashley said. She knew Brandy from her maths class. But she had never heard her tell any jokes.

"Welcome, girls," Mrs. Pritchard announced

from the stage. "Thank you for coming to our annual Queen of Fools tryouts. I'd like to introduce our first comic. Please welcome Brandy Oliver from Marble Manor!"

Ashley applauded with the audience as Brandy ran past her onto the stage.

"I don't know anything about sports," Brandy joked. "I thought a quarterback was when I got change!"

*Good one,* Ashley thought. *But I hope my jokes are better.*

"My family is not very athletic," Brandy said. "My uncle is so clumsy, he trips over his cordless phone."

Ashley watched as Brandy went on with her act.

"You were a great audience," Brandy said after a few more jokes. She ran off the stage.

Ashley jumped up and down with excitement. She was next. And she really felt that her jokes were as funny as Brandy's were. Maybe they were funny enough to win!

"Thank you, Brandy," Mrs. Pritchard said. "And now here's our next candidate. Let's hear it for Ashley Burke from Porter House!"

*It's show time!* Ashley thought. She burst through the curtain. With a big smile she strolled up to the microphone and faced the audience.

"Hi, guys," Ashley said. Dozens of faces were watching her – waiting for her to be funny. Her heart started to beat a little faster. *I can do this*, she thought.

Ashley gave the audience a bright smile. "So, did you hear the one about . . ." she stopped for a second. She blinked. "About . . ."

*What is the rest of that joke?* she wondered as she looked out into the audience.

Ashley cleared her throat. "Why don't I try another one," she said into the microphone. "How about the one where . . . um . . ." Ashley felt her face turn red.

She tried to run through her routine in her mind. But it was hopeless. She couldn't remember *any* of her jokes!

# CHAPTER EIGHT

*Oh, no,* Mary-Kate thought as she watched Ashley freeze onstage. *I have to help her.*

"Hey, Ashley!" Mary-Kate yelled out. "Tell them the one about the gargoyles."

"Right," Ashley said. She put one hand on her hip and smiled at the audience. "Did anyone check out the gargoyles in the dining hall? They're so ugly, they make the onions cry!"

Mary-Kate let out a big laugh. So did the rest of the auditorium.

"I was going to bring everyone today's oatmeal," Ashley went on, "but they're using it to cement the new basketball court!"

The audience cracked up again.

"Speaking of sports, what do baseball players eat on?" Ashley asked. "Home plates!"

Ashley went on with her act. With each joke, the audience laughed harder and harder.

"You've been a super audience," Ashley said when the act was over. "And remember my motto: Save the trees – ban homework!"

The audience cheered and clapped. Mary-Kate stood up and cheered the loudest.

"That was the very funny Ashley Burke from Porter House," Mrs. Pritchard said. "Now let's give a hand for Kimberly Klaster from Marble Manor!"

Mary-Kate applauded politely as a girl in a cow-girl suit and boots clunked onto the stage.

"I think Ashley is definitely going to win," Mary-Kate whispered to Phoebe.

"I think you're right," Phoebe whispered back.

Five more girls performed after the cowgirl. Their jokes were funny. But Ashley's were way funnier.

Finally it was time for the moment of truth. It was time to pick the Queen of Fools!

Mrs. Pritchard took the microphone. She had a sheet of paper in her hands. "Can we have the eight contestants back onstage, please?" she asked.

Ashley filed onto the stage along with the other

girls. Mary-Kate could see that her sister's fingers were crossed.

"And now," Mrs. Pritchard said, "your applause will determine our next Queen of Fools."

Mrs. Pritchard asked each contestant to step forward one at a time. When Ashley stepped forward, Mary-Kate went wild. So did everyone else!

"Ash-ley! Ash-ley! Ash-ley!" the crowd cheered.

"There's no question about it," Mrs. Pritchard said. "Ashley Burke is this year's Queen of Fools!"

Mary-Kate watched as Mrs. Pritchard placed a gold crown on Ashley's head.

Ashley shook Mrs. Pritchard's hand. Then she ran off the stage and straight to Mary-Kate.

"Way to go!" Mary-Kate said, giving her sister a hug.

"Thanks," Ashley said. "Now Ross and I will be King and Queen of Fools. Isn't that perfect?"

Mrs. Pritchard took the microphone. "I have one more announcement to make," she said. "From now on, all the chocolate machines in the student union will be filled with granola bars instead of chocolate."

"Yes!" someone cheered from the back of the audience. Mary-Kate knew it was Lily without even looking. Everyone else in the auditorium began to quietly complain.

"No more chocolate in the chocolate machines!"

Campbell gasped. "She took it way too far this time!"

"I agree," Mary-Kate said. "Come on. Let's all go talk to her right now."

Ashley waved goodbye to Mary-Kate as she was swept away by students who wanted to congratulate her. Mary-Kate and her teammates headed up the aisle towards Lily.

"Hey guys!" Mary-Kate and her friends were stopped by three girls from Porter House – Christy Stanford, Lynn Chang and Robin Sullivan.

"Isn't this exciting?" Christy asked. "The Queen of Fools is from Porter House."

"When are you going to pull your prank so we can win the furniture, too?" Lynn asked Mary-Kate.

"You *have* come up with a prank already, right?" Robin chimed in.

"Of course," Mary-Kate blurted out. "This was the plan all along. To let the other teams think they're ahead. Then we move in from behind to take the lead."

"Cool," Robin said. "Can't wait to find out what the prank is." The three girls walked away.

"So what is our next prank going to be?" Elise asked.

Mary-Kate thought for a minute. "Well, there's . . .

um, maybe . . . " But she couldn't come up with anything. "I can't believe it," she cried. "I've got April Fools' block and time is running out!"

*Wait a second,* Mary-Kate thought. *Time! Why didn't I think of it before?* "That's it," she said.

"What's it?" Phoebe asked.

Mary-Kate motioned for everyone to lean in. "It's the oldest trick in the book, but it always gets a laugh," she explained. "We can sneak into one of the dorms and turn back everyone's alarm clocks!"

"How far back will we set the clocks?" Phoebe asked.

"Just enough so that the girls will miss the morning announcement and breakfast," Mary-Kate explained. "And we'll greet them in the front hall with trays of muffins and orange juice."

Elise nodded. "I like it! I like it!"

"Which dorm should we play the prank on?" Phoebe asked.

"How about Marble Manor?" Campbell suggested. "We tried to play our last prank on Phipps."

"Sure, why not?" Mary-Kate said. "Now, here's the plan. Tonight after lights-out we'll dress in black and sneak over to Marble Manor."

"If we're super-sneaky, no one should catch us," Elise said.

"So what do you say?" Mary-Kate asked. "Think this will put us back in the game?"

"Way back in the game," Campbell said. "Maybe we'll even win."

"Great," Mary-Kate cried. She couldn't wait to score!

"So how did it go?" Mary-Kate whispered. She was standing in the ground floor hallway of Marble Manor late on Thursday night. She shone her flashlight on each of her teammates. "I want full reports!"

"Well, Lindsey Falkner sleeps with a teddy bear," Phoebe announced.

"Not *that* kind of report," Mary-Kate whispered. "Did everyone set back the alarm clocks?"

All the girls nodded.

"I can't believe we pulled it off," Mary-Kate whispered. "We are so going to win!"

"There's just one room left." Cheryl pointed to a door behind Mary-Kate.

Mary-Kate turned around. Her eyes landed on a door plastered with a huge petition that read Save the Rainforest. And it was signed first by Lily!

"Guess what?" Mary-Kate whispered. She pointed to the petition. "This is Lily's room."

"Hey, I forgot she lived here!" Phoebe whispered. "Now we can get back at her for all the stuff she's been changing around."

"So who's going to turn Lily's clock back?" Elise asked.

"I'll do it," Mary-Kate said. "It's the least I can do as your captain." She pressed her ear to Lily's door. "Lily snores," she whispered. "At least we know she's asleep."

After a round of good-lucks, Mary-Kate turned the doorknob. Very carefully, she opened the door and stepped inside. Then she zeroed in on Lily's alarm clock.

Mary-Kate held her breath as she carefully grabbed the clock. By the light of her flashlight she began to set it back.

"Hey!" Lily cried.

Mary-Kate froze with the clock in her hands. She was caught!

# CHAPTER NINE

Mary-Kate slowly turned to face Lily.

"So you think you're too good to save the bull seals?" Lily mumbled. Then she rolled over and started snoring again.

Mary-Kate sighed with relief. Lily was just talking in her sleep!

Mary-Kate set down the alarm clock, quickly tiptoed out of the room, and shut the door. "I did it," she whispered to her teammates.

The team laughed and ran out of the dorm. They stopped running when they were outside.

"We finally pulled one off!" Elise said.

Mary-Kate nodded. "A prank that will prove who the best pranksters are," she added.

\*  \*  \*

On Friday morning, the Porter House April Fools' team gathered in the front hall of Marble Manor with a tray of muffins and juice – and one bowl of oatmeal.

"If I calculate correctly," Mary-Kate said, "their alarm clocks should have rung about ten minutes ago."

"Which means they've already discovered they've overslept," Elise said excitedly.

"I'd better start rolling," Phoebe said. She had brought her video camera along to record the event. "Mrs. Pritchard is going to need proof of our prank."

One by one the Marble Manor girls began to stumble into the front hall.

"April fools!" Mary-Kate and her team chanted.

"April fools?" Lindsey Falkner groaned. She grabbed a muffin. "Very funny, you guys."

"What's going on?" a woman's voice called out.

"Mrs. Pritchard!" Mary-Kate cried. "What are you doing here?"

"I came to see why an entire dorm didn't make it to morning announcements today," Mrs. Pritchard replied.

"It was because of our prank," Cheryl said.

"Yeah," Campbell joined in. "We turned back everyone's alarm clock!"

"We were even going to tape it for you and everything," Phoebe added, holding up the video camera.

Mrs. Pritchard looked at the bewildered girls streaming down the stairs. Then she laughed. "Good job, Porter House. Your prank might just be a winner!"

Mary-Kate watched Mrs. Pritchard leave the dorm. *There's one girl we haven't seen yet,* she thought, glancing down the hall. The door with the Save The Rainforest petition was still closed.

"What happened to Lily?" Mary-Kate asked her teammates. The girls shrugged.

Mary-Kate went over to Lily's door and pressed her ear against it. She could hear someone muttering and stuff being tossed around.

"Is she up?" Elise asked.

The door flew open. A frantic Lily stared at Mary-Kate and her friends. "I'm late!" she cried.

"April fools!" the team chanted.

"We knew you'd miss breakfast," Mary-Kate said. "So we brought you some oatmeal. Plain, of course."

Lily's mouth dropped open. "You set back my alarm clock on purpose?" she asked.

Mary-Kate nodded. "That was the plan."

"Well, I didn't miss just breakfast," Lily cried. "I

missed a makeup exam. Wait until I tell my mother about this!"

"Did you see that look in Lily's eyes?" Cheryl asked as she picked at a tuna fish sandwich. "She was really angry."

The girls were having lunch in the dining hall. They couldn't get over their mistake.

"When Lily tells her mom what we did, we'll probably get in big trouble," Mary-Kate groaned.

Ashley put an arm around Mary-Kate. "Come on," Ashley said. "What's the worst Lily's mom can do? She'll probably make Mrs. Pritchard lecture the teams on being more careful. That's all."

"Speaking of The Head," Campbell said in a low voice, "here she comes now. And she's not smiling."

Mary-Kate watched a grim Mrs. Pritchard enter the dining hall. She called for attention.

"I'm afraid I have some bad news," Mrs. Pritchard began. "Due to a prank that interfered with an important test – the April Fools' Day contest is cancelled."

"That's not fair!" a girl from the Phipps team yelled.

"But we think we were in the lead," a team member from Marble Manor groaned.

"What about the new furniture?" someone else called out.

Soon the entire dining hall was buzzing with complaints.

Mary-Kate shrank down into her seat. *This is all my fault,* she thought miserably. *I've ruined April Fools' Day for everyone!*

# CHAPTER TEN

"This stinks," Ashley told her sister later in art class. "Now none of the dorms get the new furniture."

"And the worst part is," Mary-Kate said, sloshing her brush in a jar of blue paint, "the whole stupid thing was my fault!"

Ashley shook her head. "That's not true. You were part of a team, remember?"

"But I was the captain," Mary-Kate explained. She tilted her head as she studied her self-portrait. "Where do you think I should paint the word Loser?"

"Cheer up, Mary-Kate," Ashley said. "There must be something you can do to make it better."

"Getting the competition back on is the only thing left for me to do," Mary-Kate said. "But I don't have a clue how to do it." She sighed. "Plus I feel really bad about making Lily miss her test. I know she's annoying, but I didn't want to get her in trouble."

"Why don't you apologise?" Ashley said as she brushed some paint on her canvas.

"I should definitely do that," Mary-Kate said. "I'll go right after class. But she might not want to listen to me. You have no idea how angry she was when she found out we played a trick on her."

"Yo!" Jeremy said. Ashley turned to look at her cousin. He was walking away from his easel towards her, with something behind his back.

"How's it going, Ms. Queen of Fools?" Jeremy asked.

"Great," Ashley said. "I can't wait to tell Ross that I'm queen."

"So you haven't heard, then?" Jeremy asked.

"Heard what?" Ashley replied.

"Well . . . Ross was funny. But not funny enough. He isn't the king," Jeremy said.

"What?" Ashley almost dropped her paintbrush. She stared at Jeremy. "Then, who is?"

Jeremy grinned. He pulled a crown from behind his back and plopped it on his head. "I am!"

Ashley's mouth fell open. "You've got to be

kidding me," she said.

"Long live King Jeremy," Jeremy said with a grin. He paused. "King Jeremy. I like the sound of that!"

Mary-Kate shook her paintbrush at Jeremy. "You told Ashley that everyone was going to vote for Ross," she complained.

"Whoops." Jeremy shrugged. "I must have forgotten that I was running, too. And I'm way funnier than Ross is."

"You tricked me!" Ashley cried. "You told me Ross was going to be king just so that I'd try out."

"But why would you want Ashley to be queen, Jeremy?" Mary-Kate asked.

"Can't it be because I love my cousin?" Jeremy asked.

"No," both girls answered.

"Well, the reason doesn't matter," Jeremy went on. "All that matters is that you won, just like you wanted." He adjusted his crown and went back to his easel.

Ashley twisted her paintbrush so hard, it almost snapped. "Mary-Kate!" she wailed. "I was supposed to hang out at the banquet with my boyfriend, not my cousin."

"Don't think about Jeremy," Mary-Kate said.

"Think about the beautiful dress you're going to wear the night of the banquet. You picked one out already, right?"

Ashley nodded. "My black dress with velvet trim."

"And that awesome gold crown," Mary-Kate added.

"That's true." A smile spread across Ashley's face. She was starting to feel a little better about things.

"Okay, okay." Ashley laughed. "So it will still be fun to be queen." She watched as Mary-Kate turned to her self-portrait and added some paint. "Thanks for cheering me up," Ashley went on. "And don't worry. I'm sure you'll find a way to cheer up Lily, too!"

Mary-Kate knocked on Lily's door that afternoon. "Lily?" she called. "Are you in there?"

The door opened. "May I help you?" Lily asked in a frosty voice.

"Hi," Mary-Kate said. "I was hoping we could talk."

"About what?" Lily asked. She narrowed her eyes. "Is this another April Fools' prank?"

Mary-Kate shook her head. "I just wanted to tell

you that I'm really sorry," she said. "I thought you would miss the morning announcement and breakfast like everyone else. I didn't know you would miss your test."

Lily sighed. "Well, thanks for the apology," she said. "At least I know you weren't doing it to be mean. A lot of people haven't been that nice to me since I've been here."

Mary-Kate paused. "Well, I think people are a little angry about all the changes you've been making," she admitted.

Lily tilted her head. "At my old school, everyone loved when I would fight for change. I thought everyone here would, too."

"But you changed all that stuff without asking any of us," Mary-Kate explained. "And we liked it the way it was."

"But don't you see," Lily went on. "The soap, the shampoo, and even the flavoured oatmeal all had some pretty yucky chemicals in them. All-natural products are so much better for you – and the environment, too." She sighed. "At my old school, we even started a club!"

"So, maybe you can start a club here, too!" Mary-Kate said. "That way everyone who wants to can decide on the changes that should be made together."

Mary-Kate glanced into the room and saw a 4-You poster taped to the wall. "You like 4-You?" she asked. "So do I! I even have an autographed picture of 4-You hanging over my desk in my room."

"Wow," Lily said, waving Mary-Kate into the room. "That's so cool. I'm in their official fan club."

Mary-Kate smiled. Who would have thought she and Lily would have something in common? And it was great that Lily cared so much about people and the environment. "I'm glad I came over," she said.

"So am I," Lily replied. "I had no idea people felt that way about me. Is there anything I can do to make it better?"

Mary-Kate thought for a minute. "I don't think so," she replied. Then she hesitated. "Wait a minute. Maybe there is something you can do! Can you convince your mother to bring back the April Fools' Day competition?"

Lily leaned back against her desk. "I'll see what I can do!"

That night at dinner Mary-Kate could hardly eat. She couldn't stand the suspense! Had Lily already talked to her mother?

"Do you think Mrs. Vanderhoff will bring back the competition?" Phoebe asked, spearing a baby carrot.

"We'll see," Cheryl said. "But I wouldn't get our hopes up."

"Hey, look," Campbell said. "Here comes Mrs. Pritchard and Mrs. Vanderhoff now!"

"And Lily!" Phoebe cried.

Mary-Kate watched Mrs. Pritchard walk to the front of the dining hall with Mrs. Vanderhoff. Lily sat at a nearby table.

"I won't be long, girls," Mrs. Pritchard said. "I just want to announce that the April Fools' competition is back on. So may the best team win."

*I can't believe it,* Mary-Kate thought. *Lily did it!*

"Ye-es!" Cheryl cried.

"Porter House still has a chance to win!" Elise cheered.

"However," Mrs. Prichard went on, "since Porter House broke one of the rules by interfering with schoolwork, I'm sorry to say that their team is disqualified."

# CHAPTER ELEVEN

"And let it be known," Ashley said into her mirror, "that as your Queen of Fools, I declare each and every day April Fools' Day!"

Ashley blew kisses into the mirror. It was finally April Fools' Day. She was alone in her room dressing up her outfit for the banquet.

Ashley smoothed down her black dress with the velvet trim. "Maybe Phoebe will lend me her satin gloves," she murmured. "But what else should I wear?"

Ashley yanked a pair of Phoebe's vintage high-heels from her wardrobe and tried them on. *Hmmm*, she thought, looking in the mirror. *It still needs something else.*

*Every queen needs jewellery,* she decided. "Gold, of course," Ashley said. She glanced at the crown on her dressing table. "To match my gold crown."

Ashley picked a pretty gold necklace out of her jewellery box and put it on. Then she stared at her reflection in the mirror. Now she could definitely pass for a queen!

Ashley sighed. *If only Ross could have been king,* she thought. She had been so busy the past few days that she hadn't seen Ross at all.

A knock on the door made her jump. "Who is it?" Ashley called.

"It's Ms. Viola," the housemother called back. "There's a Harrington boy downstairs. He said he has something to give to you."

*Who could it be?* Ashley wondered. She bounded down the stairs to the main floor. She groaned when she saw Jeremy.

"Hey!" Jeremy said. A big black bag was draped over his arm. "I came by to drop off your queen costume."

"Costume?" Ashley repeated. "What costume?"

"Whoops," Jeremy said. He smacked his forehead. "I must have forgotten to tell you."

Ashley dragged the long bulky bag off Jeremy's arm and put it over her own. *Maybe having a cos-*

*tume wouldn't be so bad,* she thought. *It could be a royal robe.*

"What does it look like?" Ashley asked.

"Don't worry," Jeremy said with a grin. "It's perfect for you."

Ashley hugged the garment bag. It felt thick and plush, just like a royal robe would feel! "Okay," she said. "I'll see you tonight at the banquet."

"Yup," Jeremy said. "And don't get jealous – but I get to cut the first piece of the traditional jelly roll. That is – before I eat it."

"I'll try not to get too jealous," Ashley replied. She closed the door and raced up the stairs. As she ran she heard a soft jingling sound coming from the bag.

*That's weird,* Ashley thought. Why would there be bells on a queen's costume?

Ashley entered her room and carefully laid the bag across her bed. Then she slowly unzipped it – and gasped. It wasn't a royal robe at all.

"It's – a jester suit!" Ashley cried. She examined the goofy outfit. There was a hat that sprouted into four points, with bells attached to each point. The rest of the costume looked like a pair of green, red, blue and yellow footsie pyjamas with pointy feet.

"No! No! No!" Ashley wailed.

The door opened a crack and Mary-Kate peeked inside. "Ashley?" she asked. "Are you okay?"

"This is what I have to wear to the banquet tonight." Ashley waved the jester suit in front of Mary-Kate.

"Whoa," Mary-Kate said as she took in the suit. "What happened to your velvet dress? And your crown?"

"This is getting worse and worse," Ashley said. "Not only do I have to go to the banquet with my cousin, but I have to wear this stupid outfit! How could Jeremy do this to me?"

"Did you forget who you're talking about?" Mary-Kate asked. "Jeremy, the guy who made me hand-feed him hot dogs so he'd give me back my diary? I wish we could play a prank on him."

Ashley smiled as an idea formed in her head. "I think we can, Mary-Kate. And I have the perfect plan."

# CHAPTER TWELVE

"I can't believe Ashley came up with such a brilliant idea," Mary-Kate said excitedly. "We've been so bummed about being out of the competition. This prank will definitely get our spirits up."

Ashley's jester cap jingled as she walked with Mary-Kate and her teammates to the Backward Banquet.

"What do you mean, you can't believe it?" Ashley asked with a grin. "I *am* the Queen of Fools!"

"So how did you pull it off?" Elise asked.

"This afternoon I filled a long, fat balloon with yellow mustard," Mary-Kate explained. "Then I blew up the balloon."

"Then I frosted the balloon with vanilla cream and coconut flakes," Ashley said, "making it look exactly like the traditional April Fools' jelly roll."

"So when Jeremy sticks the knife into this cake to cut the first slice," Mary-Kate said, "ka-blam! The King of Fools will be the King of Goo."

"That is so funny," Phoebe said. "But how did you switch the real cake with the mustard-filled balloon?"

"The real cake was already in the dining room," Ashley explained. "So while Mary-Kate kept the kitchen staff busy, I made the switch."

As they entered the dining hall, Ashley hardly recognised it. Rubber chickens hung from the ceiling. The gargoyles wore goofy wigs and bow ties. Even the portraits of the ex-headmistresses were decorated with fake noses and moustaches.

Twitching across the colourfully decorated tables were silly windup toys and chattering teeth.

"April Fools' rules," Mary-Kate declared.

Ashley spotted two tall chairs with red velvet cushions at the front of the room. *That must be my throne,* she realised.

Tons of White Oak and Harrington kids were laughing and tossing streamers at each other. Mrs. Pritchard was sitting at the front of the room with several women in suits. Next to them was a long table filled with food.

"Who are those people?" Ashley asked.

Mary-Kate shrugged. "I have no idea."

Mrs. Pritchard held up her hands for attention. Everyone settled down. "Students," she called, "I would like to welcome our special guests to this year's banquet – the members of the board of trustees."

"So, that's who they are," Ashley whispered as everyone applauded. She turned and saw Jeremy standing on the side of the dining hall. He grinned at her.

*You just wait, Jeremy,* Ashley thought.

"And next I want to welcome all of you to the Backward Banquet," Mrs. Pritchard went on. "For those of you who walked in backwards, well done!"

Ashley felt someone tap her shoulder. She turned and saw Ross standing behind her.

"Hey," Ross said, smiling. "You make a cute jester."

"Thanks," Ashley said. "But it would have been better if you were king. Or if I were wearing something else."

"I was going to ask you how you felt about wearing the costume when we were in the student union," Ross said, "but I didn't get a chance."

"How did you know about it?" Ashley asked.

"It's a tradition," Ross said. "Nobody told you?"

Ashley shook her head. "I had no idea," she said. Then she smiled. "Well, at least this evening can't get any worse, right?"

Ross groaned. "Oh, Ashley," he said. "I have to tell you something else. Something you're not supposed to know."

"What is it?" Ashley asked.

"Jeremy is going to play a prank on you tonight," Ross explained. "He wants to throw a pie in your face."

"A pie in my face!" Ashley shouted. "You've got to be kidding me."

"Nope," Ross replied. "So I'd watch out if I were you."

"Thanks," Ashley said. "I'd better figure out where Jeremy is hiding that pie while I still have time."

Ashley walked over to the food table. There weren't any pies on the tabletop. "Where could he be hiding a pie?" she wondered. She checked underneath the table. Then she looked behind the thrones. Nope. No pies anywhere.

"And now," Mrs. Pritchard announced, "I'd like to introduce our king and queen of fools – Jeremy and Ashley Burke!"

Ashley slowly made her way to the front of the dining hall. Jeremy stood next to her, with his hands behind his back.

"Let me see your hands," Ashley snapped.

Jeremy slowly brought around his hands. Ashley got ready to duck.

"Here you go," Jeremy said. He handed Ashley a bunch of goofy fake flowers. "I wanted to give you these for being such a good sport about the costume."

"Um, thanks, Jeremy," Ashley said, surprised. She took the flowers. *Did he change his mind about playing a prank on me?* she wondered.

"Isn't that sweet," Mrs. Pritchard commented.

"I guess," Ashley said.

"I love doing nice things for my cousin." Jeremy put an arm around Ashley.

Ashley narrowed her eyes. Jeremy *had* to be up to something. He was never that nice!

"We'll begin our festivities," Mrs. Pritchard said, "by having the Queen of Fools release the balloons!"

"What do I do, Mrs. Pritchard?" Ashley asked.

"Just pull on this rope." Mrs. Pritchard gestured to a white cord behind the table. "The balloons will be released from a net on the ceiling."

Ashley smiled at the kids sitting at the long tables. Then she turned and pulled on the rope.

*SPLAT!*

A pie fell on her head!

The dining hall exploded with laughter as whipped cream dripped down Ashley's face.

"April fools!" Jeremy yelled. He laughed so hard he bent over and grabbed his stomach.

"Jeremy, that wasn't very nice," Mrs. Pritchard said. But Ashley could tell she was trying not to laugh, too.

"Sorry, Mrs. Pritchard," Jeremy replied. "I couldn't stop myself." He reached out and spooned some whipped cream off Ashley's face and ate it. "Mmmm, banana!"

Ashley wanted to scream. But she took a deep breath instead. She would have her payback soon enough.

"And now," Mrs. Pritchard began, "we will cut the traditional jelly roll."

Ashley smiled at Mary-Kate. Their moment of revenge was about to come!

A bunch of kids played kazoos as a fanfare.

"Usually the King of Fools cuts the jelly roll," Mrs. Pritchard said. "But tonight I would like to ask one of our special guests to do the honour."

"No way!" Jeremy complained, crossing his arms.

"No way!" Ashley gasped. Jeremy *had* to cut the cake.

"So please welcome the new head of the board," Mrs. Pritchard said. "Mrs. Celia Vanderhoff!"

# CHAPTER THIRTEEN

Mary-Kate stared in horror as Mrs. Vanderhoff walked over to the table with the jelly roll on it.

"Thank you, Mrs. Pritchard," Mrs. Vanderhoff said. She picked up a huge knife from the table. "This is quite an honour." Mrs. Vanderhoff began to lower the knife into the balloon.

Mary-Kate jumped up from her seat. "Wait!" she cried out. She saw Ashley cover her eyes.

*KA-BLAM!*

Mary-Kate gasped. Mrs. Vanderhoff was covered with goo. Whipped cream was splattered in her hair. Jelly dripped down her face. And her clothes were covered with bright yellow mustard!

"I can't believe this happened," Mary-Kate said,

her voice quivering. "I just can't believe it."

"How did another one of our pranks backfire?" Elise cried.

"You guys did that?" Lily asked. She pointed to her mustard-coated mother.

"It was a huge mistake, Lily," Mary-Kate explained. She watched as jelly dripped off Mrs. Vanderhoff's chin.

"Well," Mrs. Vanderhoff said in a cool voice. "This was an unpleasant surprise."

"Mrs. Vanderhoff!" Mrs. Pritchard cried. "I'm so sorry. I don't know how this happened."

"Perhaps that's the problem," Mrs. Vanderhoff snapped. "You obviously don't know how to control your students, Mrs. Pritchard."

*Oh, no*, Mary-Kate thought. *She's taking it out on poor Mrs. Pritchard.*

"Now, if you'll excuse me, I need to wash off this mess," Mrs. Vanderhoff said. She marched out of the dining hall, followed by the other board members.

"I'll be in my office if anyone needs me," Mrs. Pritchard called after them, and left the room, too.

Mary-Kate and her team ran over to Ashley. "Ashley!" she cried. "What are we going to do?"

"I don't know." Ashley pulled her jester's cap off her head. "This is all my fault."

"Come on." Mary-Kate sighed. "We have to go to Mrs. Pritchard's office to confess."

Mary-Kate, Ashley and their friends left the dining hall. They trudged across the campus to Mrs. Pritchard's office.

"All we wanted to do was be better pranksters than Olivia Farquar," Elise moaned. "You know, be a part of White Oak history."

"Well, we'll probably go down in White Oak history as the worst pranksters ever," Mary-Kate replied.

The girls reached the main building and went inside. The door to Mrs. Pritchard's office was closed, but through the glass Mary-Kate could see the board members inside, talking to the head-mistress.

"I hope they go easy on Mrs. Pritchard," Cheryl said. A few minutes later, the door opened and the board members marched out of the office. Their faces were serious.

Mary-Kate stuck her head into Mrs. Pritchard's office. "Mrs. Pritchard?" she asked. "Can we talk to you?"

Mrs. Pritchard was sitting behind her desk. She looked over her glasses and nodded.

Mary-Kate took a deep breath. "We just want to

say that we were responsible for the exploding jelly roll."

"Is that right?" Mrs. Pritchard asked.

"It was my idea," Ashley admitted. "I wanted to get back at Jeremy for not telling me about this stupid jester suit."

"But we had no idea Mrs. Vanderhoff would cut the jelly roll," Elise added quickly.

"Poor Mrs. Vanderhoff," Mrs. Pritchard added. "But it really doesn't matter any more."

"It doesn't?" Campbell asked.

"Why not?" Cheryl added.

"Because from now on there'll be some changes at White Oak," Mrs. Pritchard said.

"I know," Mary-Kate said. "They're doing away with April Fools' Day at White Oak for good. Right?"

"Wrong," Mrs. Pritchard said. "They're doing away with me for good."

Mary-Kate stared at Mrs. Pritchard. "What are you talking about?" she asked.

"You see, girls," Mrs. Pritchard said. She folded her hands on her desk. "I've been fired."

"Fired?" Mary-Kate gasped.

"You can't be!" Ashley cried.

"It's true," Mrs. Pritchard said. "The board feels

that I can't control the students. And after the jelly roll incident, they seem to be right."

Mary-Kate felt horrible. Mrs. Pritchard was an awesome headmistress!

"We won't let this happen, Mrs. Pritchard," Ashley said. "We'll picket in front of the board's office with huge protest signs."

"And we'll get our parents to write letters," Cheryl said.

"And if that doesn't work," Phoebe added, "we'll have a sit-in. Just like they did in the 1960s."

Mrs. Pritchard stared at the girls one by one. Then she began to laugh. "All of you fell for it!"

"Huh?" Mary-Kate asked.

"April fools!" Mrs. Pritchard said, throwing her hands up in the air.

"April fools?" Ashley gulped.

Mrs. Pritchard nodded. "I couldn't get through April Fools' Day without playing at least one prank, could I?"

Mary-Kate breathed a sigh of relief. They hadn't lost their Head after all!

"I think your prank is the best one this year, Mrs. Pritchard," Ashley said.

"Yeah." Mary-Kate laughed. "Olivia Farquar, step aside."

"Now let's all get back to the banquet," Mrs. Pritchard said. "I've got to announce the winners of the competition."

"So is Mrs. Vanderhoff really angry?" Phoebe asked.

"Don't worry, girls," Mrs. Pritchard said. "I calmed her down."

The group made their way back across campus to the dining hall. When they entered the room the kids were already feasting on dinner.

Mary-Kate sat next to Lily and explained everything.

"Maybe you'll win an honorary prize." Lily giggled. "For the team with the most pranks that backfired!"

After dinner, Mrs. Pritchard got up to speak.

"The time has come to announce the winning April Fools' team," she said. "And this year the grand prize goes to . . . "

The whole dining room was silent. Mary-Kate saw the girls from Marble Manor and Phipps lean forward in their chairs.

" . . . Marble Manor!" Mrs. Pritchard announced.

The girls from Marble Manor jumped up and cheered. Mary-Kate and her team applauded with everyone else.

"Oh, well," Mary-Kate said. "You can't say we didn't have fun."

"And who cares about new furniture anyway?" Phoebe said. "I kind of like our old chairs. Very retro."

"And I'm sure the rest of the dorm will forgive us," Cheryl added. "Eventually."

"I guess that's the end of our pranks," Mary-Kate said.

"Not quite," Ashley said. She had a smile on her face. "Check it out."

Ashley crossed over to the dessert table and picked up a triple-layer chocolate mousse cake. With the cake resting in one hand she marched straight over to Jeremy, who was sitting on his throne.

"Look," Mary-Kate cheered. "Ashley's about to—"

*SPLAT!*

The dining hall exploded with laughter as the King of Fools stood covered with cake. Wiping off her hands, Ashley strolled back to Mary-Kate and the table.

"Now our pranks are over!" Ashley declared.

Mary-Kate laughed. Ashley had finally got her revenge. And by the looks of all that chocolate on Jeremy, it was definitely sweet!

## THE BACKWARD BANQUET

By Elise Van Hook

It's time to put away your rubber chickens, trick gum and exploding peanut cans. April Fools' Day is over, folks, but it sure was one to remember!

The Backward Banquet alone will have people talking for weeks. Why? Because someone's prank left the president of the board of trustees dripping with whipped cream, jelly, and mustard. She didn't think it was funny – but everyone else did!

And while we're on the topic of food, I loved starting the meal with dessert. That should become standard dining hall practice!

But nothing topped when Mrs. Pritchard sat on a

whoopie cushion right before dinner. I don't think I've ever seen The Head turn so red. Will the guilty prankster please step forward? We all want to know who the mastermind was behind that one!

## GLAM GAB
By Ashley Burke

*Fashion expert Ashley Burke*

We're always on the lookout for the latest in cool, right? But I'll bet you didn't know that there's one trend that's been around forever.

Want to find out how to make your eyes stand out, or your skin glow brighter without a makeover? All you have to do is wear the right colours for you! Are you a Winter, Spring, Summer or Autumn? Check out our style guide below to find your best shades.

Do you have dark hair and a dark complexion? You're a Winter! Break out the bold colours like red, royal blue and black.

If you have red hair and a pale complexion, you're an Autumn. You look best in dark, muted colours, like olive green, gold and orange.

Are you sporting dark blonde or light brown hair with a medium complexion? You're a Spring. Pastels such as baby blue, mint green, and peach are the right choices for you.

And for those of you with blonde hair and a rosy complexion, you're a Summer. Stand out in bright colours like sunny yellow, hot-pink, and purple.

Hue go girl!

## FOOLED YOU!
By Mary-Kate Burke

*Sports pro Mary-Kate Burke*

Congratulations to Marble Manor – the winners of this year's April Fools' Day competition. As the captain of the Porter House team, I had lots of fun just being in the game and coming up with pranks. Plus, I learned a lot about April Fools' Day, too!

Did you know that April Fools' Day was originally a French holiday? That's right – it all began in the sixteenth century. Way back then, the start of the new year was celebrated on April the first. But in 1562, the Pope decided to change the calendar so that the new year started on January the first.

A lot of people in France didn't believe in the new calendar, so they still cele-brated New Year on April the first. But the ones who liked the new calendar called these people fools and played tricks on them. I guess the United States thought it sounded like

fun because they picked up on it, too. And that's how April Fools' Day was born!

So now here we are, hundreds of years later, still playing pranks on April the first. And thanks to our awesome White Oak tradition, first-formers will be playing pranks for many years to come!

## THE GET-REAL GIRL

Dear Get-Real Girl,

My roommate is totally annoying! Every week she redecorates our dorm room without asking me first if she can. Sometimes it's so different I don't even recognise it. I don't want to start a fight with her, but how can I get her to stop changing things around? I like my room the way it is!

Signed,
Dazed and Confused

Dear Dazed,

I have three words that hold the secret to solving your problem. Just Ask Her. Now was that so hard to figure out? Talking to

your roommate about redecorating your room shouldn't start a fight if you approach her nicely.

Tell her why what she does bothers you. And on the flipside, maybe you should let her do a little redecorating every once in a while. After all, change is good!

Signed,
Get-Real Girl

Dear Get-Real Girl,

My boyfriend's birthday is coming up and I have to buy him a present. It's the

first gift I've ever given him and I'm nervous because I don't know what to get. What's the perfect gift for a boyfriend?

Signed,
Scared to Shop

Dear Scared,

How should I know? He's your boyfriend. That's the key here – there is no perfect gift for a boyfriend because every person is different. But to figure out the perfect gift for *your* boyfriend, you have to think about what he likes. What are his hobbies? Has he mentioned anything recently that he would like to have? Maybe he's been giving you hints for what to get him all along and you didn't even know it. Listen extra-closely to your cutie and he'll probably tell you the answer!

Signed,
Get-Real Girl

## THE FIRST FORM BUZZ
By Dana Woletsky

Everyone at White Oak gets extra-sneaky around April Fools' Day. I had to use my supersnooper skills to get the gossip this month!

Can it be true that AB had to ask her cousin to come up with her routine for the Queen of Fools competition? Of course it can. There's no way AB could actually be funny on her own!

Speaking of the Queen of Fools, I heard one of the

contestants actually cried when she didn't win. Face it BO – you stink! Quit being such a baby.

And while we're on the topic of babies, what was a teddy bear doing in the sleeping arms of one of the

Marble Manor teammates? Tell me LF, do you have a dummy and blankie in your bed, too?

And last but not least – a rumour going around about *me*. People are saying that my team didn't really pull the pyjama prank. All I have to say is, if some wanna-be pranksters who shall remain nameless (Porter House) can't get their act together, that's no reason to blame another team!

# UPCOMING CALENDAR
Spring/Summer

Up for a challenge? This summer White Oak and Harrington are headed for the Islands of Hawaii, to participate in a survival programme on the beach.

Think you've got what it takes to survive? Come to the info meeting on May 6th in the student union.

I know it took forever, but another school year has gone by. It's already time to choose your dorm for next year! Bring friends and roommates to the annual dorm lottery next Saturday in the main hall.

Softball season is coming to a close. Join us at the final game on May 14th.

Mary-Kate Burke is up for MVP this year, and she needs you there in the stands to cheer her on!

I bet you're so busy studying for finals, that you forgot all about the woman in your life that's like no other – your mother! Mother's Day is fast approaching. Show

her how much you care by sending her some flowers through the White Oak Flowers Express programme.

# IT'S ALL IN THE STARS
## Spring Horoscopes

---

## Taurus
### (April 20-May 20)

One thing to know about a Taurus is to never throw her a curveball. Bulls hate change! But this month, why not branch out a little, Taurus? You know that new girl you've been meaning to talk to in school? Now's the time to strike up a conversation. And that funky haircut you've been too scared to try? Fear no more! You'll find that in the long run, letting change into your life can only lead to bigger and better things!

## Gemini
### (May 21-June 20)

Can't make up your mind this month? Whatever that important decision is that's been weighing you down, don't worry. Your friends and family are there to help you figure out the answer. And whatever choice you make – we're sure that it will be the right one!

## Cancer
### (June 21-July 22)

Hey, couch potato! It's time to get up, get out, and get moving! This month is not about being lazy. It's about enjoying the season to the fullest. Take your friends on a picnic, play an outdoor sport, or just take a long walk and breathe in the spring air. Everything is new and fresh outside – you don't want to miss it!

*PSST!* Take a sneak peek at

# TWO of a kind™
## *Diaries* ㉓
### Island Girls

Dear Diary,

I thought our trip to Hawaii was going to be my most exciting vacation yet. The plan was to survive on the beach for a week with kids from school and our guide, Tico. The past few days went well, but today is not off to a good start.

It all began when our group was eating breakfast in a big circle on the beach. We had picked tons of yummy-looking fruit to eat. And I was so hungry after all the hiking, fishing and building we had been doing, I wanted to eat it all!

"Mary-Kate, look out!" Dana Woletsky knocked the banana out of my hand just as I was about to put it in my mouth. "You don't want to eat that," she said.

I glanced at the banana in the sand. Dana was right.

Tons of tiny bugs were crawling all over it!

"Oh, gross!" I cried, grateful that I hadn't eaten the fruit. "Thanks, Dana."

"Wow . . ." My best friend, Campbell Smith, slowly shook her head. "That's the worst luck you've had so far."

"Well, I warned you about Pele," our guide, Tico, said, wagging a finger at me.

"I know, I know," I muttered. Yesterday we had hiked up a small, inactive volcano. I thought it was so cool that I snagged a tiny piece of volcanic rock as a souvenir.

But then Tico saw it and told me about the legend of Pele, the volcano goddess. He said that if I didn't leave a gift in exchange for the rock, I'd have nothing but bad luck from now on!

I didn't believe him at first. But that was before lots of bad stuff started happening to me. Could it be possible that the curse . . . is real?

Dear Diary,

No I am not on the beach playing the  survival game with everyone else. Instead I am stuck in a hotel room with my friends, Elise and Summer. And we are totally bored!

So what's the only logical thing to do when you're that bored? Order lots of room service!

"Check it out, guys," I said, flipping through the room service menu. "We can order ten kinds of ice cream in one big bowl!"

Summer turned up the 4-You song that was playing on the radio and bopped over to the armchair where I was sitting. "Sounds good to me," she said. "Can you order me some cheese fries?"

"And I wouldn't mind some veggies and dip," Elise added, as she polished her toenails on my bed.

I picked up the phone and gave the man at the front desk our order. I added a few more things from the menu, just in case we were still hungry later on.

It was a blast! We watched a movie, danced, sang, and ate until we were stuffed. We even cleaned out the mini-fridge.

Diary, how was I supposed to know that none of that stuff was covered by our vacation package? The hotel manager said that if we couldn't pay, he'd have to tell our assistant headmistress what we did. But we don't have the money. Which means only one thing. We are in big trouble!

Here's an excerpt from another great
Mary-Kate and Ashley series.

# Sweet 16
# NEVER BEEN KISSED

"You've already been out for a run, fed your dog and changed the oil on your Jeep?" I asked Jake, amused.

"Yeah! Why? What have you done this morning, Mary-Kate?" he asked, laughing. I loved that laugh. Jake was definitely the coolest guy I ever dated.

I flopped down on the living room sofa and switched the phone to my right ear. "I've . . . uh . . . yawned a lot and eaten some French toast," I admitted.

"Busy girl!" Jake joked.

"Wait!' I said, snapping my fingers. "Ashley and I also started the guest list for our sweet sixteen party."

"Oh really?" Jake asked, obviously intrigued. "Am I on that guest list?"

I bit the inside of my cheek, remembering something Ashley had said the other day – something about all-girl parties being unsophisticated. If I told Jake that we were only inviting girls would he think I was a big baby?

"I'm . . . not . . . sure," I said, stalling for time.

Jake laughed, obviously taking my answer as a flirty joke instead of the honest truth.

"Well, I'll just have to spend all my time being nice to you so that you'll decide to invite me," Jake said. "Of course, I was planning on doing that anyway."

My heart melted. Maybe, just maybe, a boy-girl party wasn't such a bad idea. Not if totally gorgeous Jake would be my date.

Maybe I'd been a little bit too quick to decide about this all-girl concept. . .

"So, I'm really looking forward to our date on Monday," Jake said. "Let's meet in the lobby after last period."

"Sounds like a plan!" I said with a grin.

"Okay," Jake said. "Bye, Mary-Kate."

The second I hung up the phone I let out a little squeal under my breath. Jake was just so – amazing!

I walked back to the kitchen, ready to reopen the all-girl party debate and shock my sister with the news that I was ready to rethink it. But Ashley was busy chatting on my mom's mobile.

"Who's she talking to?" I whispered to my father, who was reading the morning paper.

"The party planner," he whispered back.

Before I could even process this, I suddenly tuned in to what Ashley was saying.

"Yes, Wilson, we definitely want an all-girl party," she said, gripping the phone in one hand as she doodled in her notebook with the other. "And the theme is girl power."

*Uh oh*, I thought. *What is she doing?*

Ashley glanced up at me in the middle of a sentence and smiled. She dropped her pen and gave me a little thumbs-up, obviously thinking I was thrilled.

"Thanks, Wilson," Ashley said. "Bye!" She clicked off the phone and turned around in her chair to look at us, a bright smile on her face. "He loves it!" she said. "He's already got tons of ideas!"

I forced myself to smile. "That's . . . great," I said. In with girl power, out with romance. I just hoped Jake would understand. . .

# mary-kateandashley

# TWO of a kind ™

## Coming soon – can you collect them all?

HarperCollins*Entertainment*

PARACHUTE PRESS

DUALSTAR PUBLICATIONS

AOL mary-kateandashley.com
AOL Keyword: mary-kateandashley

| | | | | |
|---|---|---|---|---|
| (1) | How to Train a Boy | (0 00 714458 X) | | |
| (2) | Instant Boyfriend | (0 00 714448 2) | | |
| (3) | Too Good to be True | (0 00 714449 0) | | |
| (4) | Just Between Us | (0 00 714450 4) | | |
| (5) | Tell Me About It | (0 00 714451 2) | | |
| (6) | Secret Crush | (0 00 714452 0) | | |
| (7) | Girl Talk | (0 00 714453 9) | | |
| (8) | The Love Factor | (0 00 714454 7) | | |
| (9) | Dating Game | (0 00 714447 4) | | |
| (10) | A Girl's Guide to Guys | (0 00 714455 5) | | |

*... and more to come!*

HarperCollins*Entertainment*

DUALSTAR PUBLICATIONS

mary-kateandashley.com
AOL Keyword: mary-kateandashley

# mary-kateandashley

## *Sweet 16*

(1) *Never Been Kissed*      (0 00 714879 8)
(2) *Wishes and Dreams*      (0 00 714880 1)
(3) *The Perfect Summer*      (0 00 714881 X)

HarperCollins*Entertainment*

PARACHUTE PRESS

DUALSTAR PUBLICATIONS

mary-kateandashley.com
AOL Keyword: mary-kateandashley

# b the 1st 2 kno
# mary-kateandashley

## REGISTER 4 THE HARPERCOLLINS AND MK&ASH TEXT CLUB AND KEEP UP2 D8 WITH THE L8EST MK&ASH BOOK NEWS AND MORE.

SIMPLY TEXT SLT, FOLLOWED BY YOUR GENDER (M/F), DATE OF BIRTH (DD/MM/YY) AND POSTCODE TO: 07786277301.

SO, IF YOU ARE A GIRL BORN ON THE 12TH MARCH 1986 AND LIVE IN THE POSTCODE DISTRICT RG19 YOUR MESSAGE WOULD LOOK LIKE THIS: SLTF120386RG19.

IF YOU ARE UNDER 14 YEARS WE WILL NEED YOUR PARENTS'' OR GUARDIANS'' PERMISSION FOR US TO CONTACT YOU. PLEASE ADD THE LETTER 'G'' TO THE END OF YOUR MESSAGE TO SHOW YOU HAVE YOUR PARENTS'' CONSENT. LIKE THIS: SLTF120386RG19G.

HarperCollins*Entertainment*

PARACHUTE PRESS

DUALSTAR PUBLICATIONS

AOL mary-kateandashley.com
AOL Keyword: mary-kateandashley

# the **mary-kateandashley** brand

## Fab freebies!

You can have loads of fun with these ultra-cool Glistening Stix from the **mary-kateandashley** brand. Great glam looks for eyes, lips – or anywhere else you fancy!

All you have to do is **collect four tokens from four different books from the mary-kateandashley** brand (no photocopies, please!), send them to us with your address on the coupon below – and a groovy Glistening Stix will be on its way to you!

### Go on, get collecting and sparkle like a star!

**Real Books for Real Girls™**

It's What **YOU** Read

---

 TOKEN

Name: ...................................................................

Address: ...............................................................

..........................................................................

e-mail: .................................................................

☐ Tick here if you do not wish to receive further information about children's books.

Send coupon to: **mary-kateandashley Marketing,**
HarperCollins Publishers, 77-85 Fulham Palace Road, Hammersmith, London W6 8JB.